Snow White, Star Striker

SUE NICHOLSON

Illustrated by FLAVIA SORRENTINO

Once Upon A Time...

...there was a misty blue mountain.

Quarto is the authority on a wide range of topics.

Quarto educates, entertains and enriches the lives of our readers—enthusiasts and lovers of hands-on living.

www.quartoknows.com

Author: Sue Nicholson
Illustrator: Flavia Sorrentino
Designer: Victoria Kimonidou
Editor: Emily Pither

First Published in 2019 by QED Publishing, an imprint of The Quarto Group.
The Old Brewery, 6 Blundell Street, London N7 9BH, United Kingdom.
T (0)20 7700 6700 F (0)20 7700 8066
www.QuartoKnows.com

A catalogue record for this book is available from the British Library.

ISBN 978-1-78603-570-7

Manufactured in Shenzhen, China HH092018

9 8 7 6 5 4 3 2 1

Below the misty blue mountain
was a wild, dark forest and by the
wild, dark forest was a village.

SCHOOL

The village had a stream and a duck pond and an old red apple tree
and it was home to **Snow White** and her fairytale friends.

Snow White loved football.

She practised on her way to school...

... on her way home...

... and after dinner, before she went to bed.

She even **dreamed** about football.

Snow White played on the village football team with her friends. The team had a match coming up against the ogres from the next village and she was one of their best players.

The only problem was, she wouldn't pass the ball.

'To me!'
yelled Jack.

'Over here!'
called Goldilocks.

Snow White wanted to score **all the goals** herself.

One day, Snow White kicked the ball so far it sailed over the goalposts into Rumpelstiltskin's garden and broke his garden gnomes.

Bash!

Smash!

Crack!

Rumpelstiltskin was furious.
'Go away!' he yelled. 'Find somewhere else to play!'

'It's your fault,' said Goldilocks to Snow White. 'You were too far away to score. You should have passed the ball!'

'You're just not a team player and you're not fun to play with,' said Jack. 'You're off the team!'

Snow White still practised but it wasn't the same without her friends.

'Are you all right?' asked Griselda.

'My friends don't want me to play with them anymore - and Rumpelstiltskin is angry because I broke his gnomes!' said Snow White.

'Rumpelstiltskin isn't so bad,' replied Griselda. 'Did you know that he was good at football when he was young? He might even be able to help...'

Snow White went to see Rumpelstiltskin.
'I'm sorry for breaking your gnomes,' she said.

'I was playing football but *I* messed things up.
Will you help me play better?'

'All right,' said Rumpelstiltskin.
'I will coach you if you help me
fix my gnomes.'

'Deal!' said Snow White.

The following week, Snow White helped Rumpelstiltskin mend the gnomes, then he taught her some team tactics.

'Can you help us, too?' asked Jack and Goldilocks.

Soon, Rumpelstiltskin was coaching the whole team.

The day of the ogres football match arrived.

'Remember, you can win if you play as a team!' Rumpelstiltskin told them.

GUEST HOME

2 2

Jack scored first, but the ogres got one back. Snow White scored next, but the ogres got another.

It was 2-2 with less than a minute to go! Then Snow White got the ball.

'To me!' yelled Jack. 'Over here!' called Goldilocks.

Snow White hesitated. She still
wanted to be her team's star striker
but Goldilocks was nearer the goal.

Then she remembered
Rumpelstiltskin's words: 'Play as a team!'

Snow White took a deep breath and passed the ball
to Goldilocks, who kicked it in the net –
just as the whistle went.

Hurrah!

The Fairytale Friends had won!

'You may not have scored the winning goal, but it's more fun playing with you now,' Goldilocks told Snow White. 'And you're still a star!'

Snow White beamed.
'In this team, we're
all stars!'

Next Steps

Discussion points

Discuss with the children what the word 'teamwork' means. Talk about the importance of working together as a team to get something done and how it feels to be part of a team. Below are suggestions for discussion points about the story. These will help the children with their comprehension skills, as well as developing their understanding of teamwork.

- Snow White loved football. She even dreamed about it. Look at the illustrations on page 2.
What do they show that Snow White was dreaming about?
  - Are you part of any teams?
  - Have you ever been on a winning team? How did it feel?
- Why do you think it was important for Snow White to pass the ball to other players in the team?
  - Can you think of any ways that you've been a good team player?
- Rumpelstiltskin gave the team some advice: 'Be supportive!', 'Help each other out!', 'Play as a team!', 'Work together!'
Do you think this was useful advice for a football team?
  - Can you think of different ways that this advice could be useful at school or with your friends?
  - How can this advice help with making and keeping friends?
- How do you think Snow White felt at the end of the story? How do you think her team mates felt?
  - Do you think it's more important to win, or play as part of a team?

Make a class newspaper

Make a large newspaper using folded sheets of sugar paper. Give each child a piece of white paper and explain that you are going to make a class newspaper together. Show them an example of a newspaper where lots of writers contribute as a team effort. Discuss the important events in the last minute of the football match from the story and write some sentences on the board describing the exciting finish. Ask the children to draw a picture of Snow White's team and encourage them to write a sentence about the game underneath. They could copy one from the board or think of their own. Ask the children to work together to stick their entries into the newspaper. This can then be used to show other children or displayed in the school's book corner.